My First Time

Going to the Doctor

Kate Petty, Lisa Kopper, and Jim Pipe

Stargazer Books
Mankato, Minnesota

© Aladdin Books Ltd 2009

Designed and produced by
Aladdin Books Ltd

First published in 2009
in the United States by
Stargazer Books,
distributed by Black Rabbit Books
PO Box 3263, Mankato, MN 56002

Printed in the United States   All rights reserved

Illustrator: Lisa Kopper   Photocredits: All photos from istockphoto.com.

Library of Congress Cataloging-in-Publication Data

Petty, Kate.
  Going to the doctor / Kate Petty.
    p. cm. -- (My first time)
  Summary: When Sam visits the doctor' office for a check-up she takes his height and weight, tests his eyesight and hearing, listens to his heart and lungs, and gives him an injection.
  Includes index.
  ISBN 978-1-59604-173-8
  [1. Medical care--Fiction. 2. Physicians--Fiction.] I. Title.
  PZ7.P44814Go 2009
  [E]--dc22
                              2008015280

About this book

New experiences can be scary for young children. This series will help them to understand situations they may find themselves in, by explaining in a friendly way what can happen.

This book can be used as a starting point for discussing issues. The questions in some of the boxes ask children about their own experiences.

The stories will also help children to master basic reading skills and learn new vocabulary.

It can help if you read the first sentence to children, and then encourage them to read the rest of the page or story. At the end, try looking through the book again to find where the words in the glossary are used.

Contents

Dad is taking Sam to the doctor today.
Sam isn't ill. He is going for a check-up.

The doctor wants to make sure
that he stays healthy.

4

"Hello, Sam. The doctor is expecting you. You'll have to wait for your turn, though."

The receptionist points the way to the waiting room.

Visits to the doctor keep you healthy.

Dad and Sam find two empty chairs.
They take off their coats and scarves.

Sam has spotted a box full of toys.
Dad sits down with Jenny.

They have to wait a long time.
Jenny falls asleep. It's Sam's turn at last.

Dad puts Jenny into her stroller
and takes Sam into the doctor's office.

7

The doctor's office is full of interesting things. Why is that teddy wearing an eyepatch?

Sam takes a good look around while the doctor talks to Dad.

8

The doctor notices Sam's new shoes.
"Can you take them off yourself, Sam?
I want to see how big you've grown."
Sam undoes his shoes and kicks them off.

Sam makes himself as tall as he can. No cheating, Sam!

The doctor measures him. He's exactly three feet tall. That's more than half as tall as Dad.

Eating well helps you grow tall!

Now Sam is going to be weighed.
He steps on to a very wobbly scale.

How heavy is he? "Can you guess, Sam?
You weigh 42 pounds."

Sam is taking off his clothes
so the doctor can feel his tummy.

She thinks she can guess what he had
for breakfast. "Was it toast, Sam?"

12

She wants to know if Sam can hop.
Of course he can. Sam likes hopping.

The doctor asks him to bring her the teddy
with the eyepatch. Sam wonders why.

Next they find out how well Sam can see.
The doctor points to letters on a chart.

Pirate Sam matches the letters
with the ones on his card.

14

Can Pirate Sam hear the doctor too?
"Point to the fish, Sam,"
she says quietly.

"Now point to the boat and to the car."

Holding still helps the doctor look closely at you.

Sam has seen a stethoscope before. He has a toy one at home.

The doctor can hear his heart beating. She listens to his breathing too.

She uses a light to peer down his throat.
It's very dark down there.

It's dark in Sam's ears too.
"What's it like in Dad's ears, Sam?"

17

Dad lifts Sam comfortably on to his lap.
The doctor dabs his arm. It's cold and wet.

"This injection will stop you getting
dangerous diseases, Sam."

Sam decides he's going to be brave.
The injection hurts a bit but not much.

Soon it is over and Sam feels
very proud of himself.

Sam has gotten dressed again.
The doctor is ready for the next patient.

Sam wants to hurry home and play
with his own doctor's kit.

Now all the cuddly toys and teddies have had injections.

But none of them was half as brave as Sam!

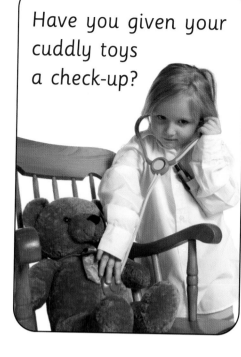

Have you given your cuddly toys a check-up?

waiting room

receptionist

weighing

measuring

eye test chart

stethoscope

light

injection

Index

Find out more

Find out more about going to the doctor at:

www.kidshealth.org
www.familydoctor.org
www.cyh.com
www.aap.org

24